DELIA'S DULL DAY

An incredibly boring story by Andy Myer

PUBLISHED BY SLEEPING BEAR PRESS

My name is Delia. You'll never guess what happened to me yesterday.

Give Up?
I'll give you a hint.

That's right!

NOTHING!!

Nothing EVER happens to me. Just look at my day yesterday....................

NOTHING
happened during my breakfast,
except I spilled some milk.

I walked past the same 16 houses I pass every day on my way to the bus stop.

And the bus ride to school was

BOOOOOOOOORRRRR

...RING

as usual.

I almost fell asleep in Mrs. Houston's math class.

Recess
was
Dull,
DULL,
DULL.

...My Jell-O squares fell into my chicken noodle soup.

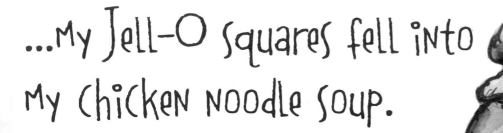

And in band I played "Yankee Doodle" 2,000 times.

...a dog BARKED at Me.

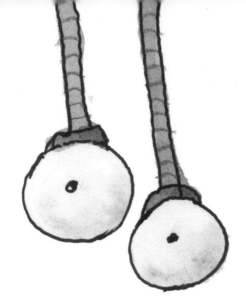

I watched

MARS INVADERS 3

for the 21st time.
Snore.

Nothing happened
when I put on
my pajamas...

...and brushed
My teeth.

And, of course, nothing **EVER** happens when I'm sleeping!

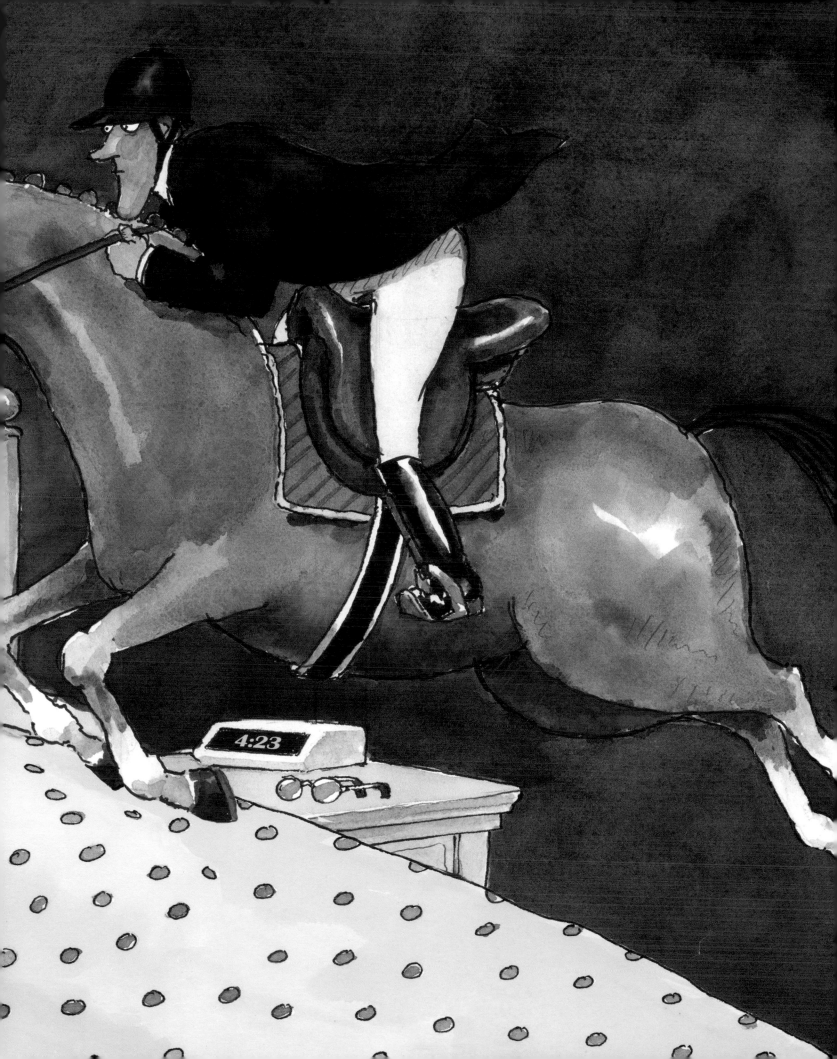

NOW do you see how
completely boring

Maybe **SOMETHING** will happen to me today.

To everyone in my precious family, who teaches me daily to look up.
— Andy

Sleeping Bear Press™

315 East Eisenhower Parkway, Suite 200

Ann Arbor, MI 48108

www.sleepingbearpress.com

Printed and bound in the United States.

10 9 8 7 6 5 4 3 2

Library of Congress Cataloging-in-Publication Data

Myer, Andy. Delia's dull day : an incredibly boring story / written and illustrated by Andy Myer.

p. cm.

Summary: "A little girl complains that her life is boring, never
realizing that amazing things are happening around her such as elephants
marching through her house, a pirate sitting behind her on the school
bus, or a submarine in her pool"–Provided by the publisher.

ISBN 978-1-58536-804-4

[1. Boredom–Fiction. 2. Humorous stories.] I. Title.

PZ7.M98125De 2012

[E]–dc23   2012007243